PASSION

(L'appassionata)

PASSION

(L'appassionata)

A Tale of Venice

Stefan Grabinski

Translated by
Miroslaw Lipinski

NoHo Press
New York

Passion

Stefan Grabinski

This translation dedicated with eternal love to
Haya Khoury

Cover illustration: Canaletto's *The Molo Looking West with the Doges' Palace*

First Polish book publication 1930.
NoHo Press paperbound edition December 2014
Translation © Miroslaw Lipinski 2014

PASSION

(L'appassionata)

A Tale of Venice

PASSION

L'APPASSIONATA

Stefan Grabinski

A fine, barely perceptible mist hung over the Cannaregio *sestiere** in the very heart of the lagoon. In the rays of a July sun that filtered through this most delicate veil, the sleepy waters of the *Canal Grande* dozed, and in them, as if conjured up from a fairy tale, peered out incredibly beautiful mansions, villas, houses and churches. Everything appeared like a golden mirage, brought to life through a sumptuous fantasy, as if it were woven from the dreams of an artist in a time of exquisite, creative exuberance.

Only a coastal wave sloshing quietly against the steps at the water's edge, only the song of a gondolier who passed by in his mournful boat, awoke me from my dazed reveries and made me aware of the joyful fact that I was, without doubt, in Venice....

Thus, infatuated with this city of Doges, drunk with the bewitching architecture and the melancholy of black, mysterious waters, I waited this wonderful morning for the *va-*

---

* A Venetian district. (Author's note.)

*poretto** that would take me to the other side of the Grand Canal.

Near me was the old San Marcuola Church from the middle of the XVII century, with its small courtyard behind the entry gate, and to the left, on the other side of a narrow *rio*, perhaps the most splendid seat of the Doges, the Vendramin Calergi Palace, the very same place where the great creator of the *Nibelungen* breathed his last. Just as my eyes were wandering over the façade, to read the motto: *"Non nobis—Domine—Non nobis,"* a long whistle from the small steamer was heard, piercing a little roughly the silence of the hour.

And so, throwing one more glance at the chaplet of the palace, I got onto the gangway, and in a moment I was already sitting at the stern of the boat.

"Avanti!" the helmsman gave the call through a tube to the pit of the boiler room, and the *vaporetto*, freed from imprisonment, began to part the lazy waters with its prow.

My journey was not going to last long: I would be getting off at the nearest stop, at San Stae. The boat passed the former house of the patrician Theodore Correr and the Museo Cívido founded by him, it went by the old granary of the Republic, the palaces Erizzo, Grimani della Vida and Fontana, and, reaching the Palazzo Tron, turned its bow to the right toward the shore.

"Ferma!" came the command from the tower in the middle of the *vaporetto*.

---

* A water tram. (Author's note.)

The whir of the machinery abated, the work of the boiler ceased, and the steamer, pulled to the side of the pontoon by a line, fraternized once again in the haven of a temporary embrace.

Successfully squeezing through the throng of passengers, I stood on the boulevard. From here to the Galleria d'Arte Moderna at the Pesaro Palace, the aim of my trip, was not far. I walked the short, lissome span of the *ponticello** over the Mocenigo *rio* and found myself on the Fondamenta Pesaro.

At this morning hour it was strangely quiet, and the splashing of waves, lazily penetrating on the mossy steps of the terrace, could be clearly heard about the porches of the palace.

I went up to the first storey. At the entrance I was met by the gloomy and reluctant gazes of the staff, who appeared to be put out by my interrupting their *dolce far niente* to deal with a ticket.

I was let inside. The galleries were almost empty: here and there a few *stranieri*** were meandering with guide books in their hands, and a bony Miss with a pince-nez was devouring with her eyes a seductive pose of a male. My attention was absorbed by Rodin's *The Burghers of Calais*. When, after a while, I tore my eyes from the sculpture and looked into the interior of the adjacent hall, I saw by one of the paintings a beautiful young lady. Her profile, subtle but resolute, with its aquiline nose, stood out clearly against a wall lit up strongly by the sun. Her raven hair, flickering with a metallic glitter,

---

* A small bridge. (Author's note.)
** Foreigners. (Author's note.)

framed a dusky, elongated face and fiery, dark-walnut eyes. The singular, unforgettable expression of these eyes merged in that wonderfully womanly way with steely flashes of unbending will: in moments of anger these eyes would be terrible. This very beautiful, patrician head was complimented perfectly by a slender and lithe body, whose outlines peered out discreetly and temptingly through a black dress full of quiet elegance and taste. Against this refined simple and modest dress an orange scarf stood out like a flame to join in a colorful symphony with a large tea rose pinned in her hair.

"What a striking woman!" I thought, crossing into the hall. She turned, and for the first time our eyes met: hers—a little distracted, then searching, finally intrigued—mine—favorable and full of admiration. On her lips dawned the hint of a smile, and stifled by the will, it slowly vanished without a trace; her indifferent, velvety eyes graced once more Fragiacomo's painting, *Fishing Boats in a Storm*.

And then a happy accident came to my aid.

As I was passing her by with a heavy heart and a feeling of dejection, the book she was holding in her hand slipped out of her fingers and fell onto the floor next to me. With lightening speed, I bent down to reach for it and read the title: *El secreto del acueducto—por Ramon Gomez de la Serna.**

"She is Spanish," I thought, and bowing as I returned her property, I asked:

"*Dispence V. Este libro pertence a V. No es verdad?*"

She looked pleasantly surprised and, taking her book, re-

---

* *The Secret of the Aqueduct*, a novel of sex and death published in 1922. (Translator's note.)

plied in the same language:

"You speak Spanish, *señor*. Perhaps you are a fellow countryman?"

"No, *señora*," I replied, "I am a Pole, but the language of the sons of Castile is not unknown to me."

Our introductions where concluded. Then began a lively and picturesque conversation between us, because she also liked a somewhat flowery style, crafted with rich words, and I, captivated by the spell of her figure, couldn't help but choose phrases as colorful as butterfly wings.

Doña Inez de Torre Orpega, a native of Extremadura, had been a widow for several years. The greater part of the year she spent in Madrid, living at the home of an older sister who was married to a court dignitary. She came to visit Venice only in the summer months, staying with relatives. Of Poland and Polish people she knew little and with interest listened to my information about the country. When we left the picture gallery half an hour later and found ourselves on the boulevard of the Fondamenta Pesaro, we were already well acquainted with each other.

"Where are you going now, *señor*?" she asked. "It is still too early for lunch, but a splendid time for brunch. Would you care to join me at a restaurant with a view of the Ponte Rialto? I very much like to observe it in the morning hours."

I was delighted.

"It would be best," I proposed, "if we would go to Corvo Nero near the *vaporetto* stop."

"Perfect. Please give me your hand and lead me to the gondola."

I looked at her with some confusion:

"At this time I do not see any. We have to wait a while until one comes up."

She replied with silvery laughter:

"My Beppo will not allow us to wait long. Ah, he has already recognized me from a distance by my voice and is approaching us in his *Rondinella*.*"

And, indeed, around the corner of the boulevard the prow of *The Swallow* could be seen. Clinging with its black underbelly to the waters of the canal between the Pesaro Palace and the Corner della Regina, the gondola crouched there momentarily, just waiting for the call.

She introduced her boatman with an expression have serious, half *buffo*. "Beppo Gualcioni, my court *gondoliere*, is an old, longtime servant of the house of Ramorin, my relatives."

And we boarded the boat.

Doña Inez's gondola was a veritable masterpiece. Slender, graceful and agile like a frigate, with a beautifully carved bow in the shape of a swan's neck, it rocked on the waves like the cradle of a royal child. With our backs leaning against pillows of dark-green plush, under the cover of a low canopy decorated with golden fringes, which are called *felze* here, we sailed as if in infinity, listening intently to the rhythm of the paddle.

The misty veils blew away completely and under the turquoise canopy of the sky the fabulously colorful vista of the Grand Canal spread out before us. Three colors dominated:

---

* "Swallow" in Italian. (Translator's note.)

the black of the water, the white of houses, and the orange of blinds and lowered shutters. These three colors, mixed with each other and joined in a fortunate kinship in their assortment, were as if one inescapable sound, as if a mysterious expression hidden deeply somewhere in the soul of this city. And everything was imbued with this supreme, sovereign voice, everything vibrated with myriad tremors of one string—a golden mono-chord, whose name is—Venice.

As if in a dream the masterpieces of Venetian architecture passed by our boat, these lacy palaces and houses, of which almost every one boasted the chisel and brush works of great artists. The July sun gilded with copper and vermilion the proud, aristocratic frontages and pediments; it lit up the subterranean passages and colonnades permeated with the darkness of ages, and cascaded a burning caress over the green oasis of garden terraces and vines that enveloped loggias.

Our gondola floated by the Ca' d'Oro palace, the most decorative Gothic structure of the old Republic; we passed the palaces of Sagredo, Michiel dalle Colonne and Morosini, and found ourselves by the fish market. The odor of the hoary water, flowing from deep within the market, overwhelmed us with its suffocating exhalations. In the full rhythm of the morning, the *peschiera* pulsated with life and activity.

Doña Inez put a tissue to her nose and, looking at me with a smile, she breathed in its perfume scent. The gondola had already reached the harbor which contained the vegetable market. Our eyes, wearied by the brightness of the day, rested with relief on the greenery of cabbage heads, cauliflower, celery, and carrot tops.

"What a contrast between this prosaic, though very refreshing view, and the sophisticated beauty of the palaces," remarked the *Doña* from Orpega.

"Indeed," I admitted, "and I'm always struck by this whenever I pass by the Erberia market. Unfortunately, it cannot be otherwise. One cannot live with the sole contemplation of works of art. I would even say that the mixture of the prose of daily life with the poetry of art and the past is the greatest charm of this strange city."

She nodded her head in a sign of agreement. A view of the Ponte Rialto Bridge, grey and covered by the patina of centuries, opened up before us. With a few deft strokes of his paddle, Beppo turned the boat to the opposite shore and, moving along to the left side by the Fondaco dei Tedeschi, the boat glided under the arch of the bridge. In a moment I was already jumping from the gondola onto waterfront stairs, moldy from the water, to give my hand to Inez.

It was eleven in the morning. We passed the *vaporetto* station at Cerva and, keeping to the edge of the canal, entered the Riva del Carbon. The crowds were enormous. Steamers were throwing out new legions of passengers every dozen minutes. We found shelter in a peaceful corner of the Corvo Nero, a small secluded *gelateria* with a view of the Rialto. Here, under the canvas awning, *Doña* Inez seemed yet more beautiful; the deep dark circles under her eyes emphasized their sweetness and fire. I couldn't stop looking at her. And she, seeing my admiration, merely smiled at the corners of her mouth and sipped orangeade through her pearly teeth.

Her sleepy, slightly dreamy glance wandered aimlessly about the other side the channel, then turned to a group of gondolas rocking in the harbor and stopped at the Rialto Bridge.

"Does that bridge remind you a little of the Ponte Vecchio in Florence?" she asked.

"That one has three arches," I replied.

"I'm referring to the top part."

"Oh, yes, certainly," I admitted. "Both of them are built up, particularly the one in Florence."

"The shops and bazaars, these tawdry sheds pitched over the water, have something very original about them…."

"They speak to the transitory nature of twentieth century and the concise vigor of the past. Perhaps you would like to walk that way?"

"I was about to propose the same thing. Once in a while I like to stroll among such garish shops."

We left our shady hospice and soon found ourselves on the arc of the bridge. We became surrounded the atmosphere of a market hall. The narrow passage between the two rows of bazaar stalls was filled with a picturesque mass of people. Women dominated: slender, ethnic townswomen in characteristic fringed black shawls. Their graceful heads, often adorned in fiery ribbons, were bent with interest over samples of goods spread over benches and counters, while their hands, lovely with refined shape, were fingering with pleasure stacks of silk, satin and calico: capricious, fussy, busy hands.

The chaos of colors was accompanied by the chaos of odors: among the din rose up the smell of cheap perfume, the harsh odor of yuft leather and a strong symphony of spices from overseas.

One shop rejoiced in dolls while, adjoining it, was a store of personal adornments that was constantly besieged by the fair sex. The owner of this store, a broad-shouldered, middle-aged man, with a melancholic drooping mustache, tantalized with his Venetian jack-a-dandies, moving his ringed fingers along fake pearls, coral and amber or shifting from hand to hand shimmering clumps of earrings, brooches and other odds and ends.

"*Signor* Giuliano is doing splendid business as usual," noted Inez, passing by the bazaar. "He knows how to tout his merchandise. "

"Everything is shoddy and fake," I replied.

"Not necessarily," she opined. "Sometimes you can find a real jewel here and there: you only have to know what's good and distinguish the wheat from the chaff. Giuliano's shack is also a kind of *bric a brac* of antiquity. We will come back here after dinner, when the Rialto is a little less crowded. And now please escort me to the gondola. I have to return home."

Surrounded by the hubbub and shouting, we went down to the boat. Beppo, refreshed by the several glasses of beer and a portion of pasta he had partaken of in a coastal *trattoria*, was briskly untying the gondola from a pole on the boulevard. When I took off my hat and fastened my eyes on *Doña* Orpega, filled with a silent request for our next meeting, she pulled me into the interior of the gondola.

"You will accompany me to my residence."

"You are so kind," I whispered, pressing my lips to her hand.

The gondola's prow was already parting the water of the canal. We were heading back in the direction of the Cannaregio. Along the way, Inez set goals for our rendezvous in the afternoon.

"You are the newcomer here," she said, resting her marvelous head on the frame of the craft. "I want to be your *cicerone*; I want to show you all the peculiarities of the city. I myself will arrange the sequence of our trips. Do you agree?"

"With the deepest gratitude. Where do we begin?"

She smiled.

"That's a secret. You will know in the afternoon. I want to surprise you. So please expect me at four at the Ca' d'Oro. Until then!"

The gondola docked to the shore, her swan neck laying down on the mossy steps of stairs that led between columns to one of those marvelous palaces from which the dark waves of the Grand Canal are so faithfully deflected. Here Inez got off. A footman was there to present his hand, as the steps were slippery and uncertain because of the green mold on them.

"Beppo, take this gentleman to San Marcuola," she ordered upon farewell and, giving me a bewitching smile, she disappeared behind a hanging drapery into the depths of the building.

I could not wait until the anticipated hour arrived. My state of excitement, created by the joyful adventure I had gone through, was so strong that I forgot about lunch and didn't go back to my lodging near the railway station; rather,

I loitered around the canal in the area of the Golden House. I could not allow any banal event to interrupt my delightful dreams about her; I could not let any prosaic occurrence squeeze itself between my first and second meeting with this dear woman. That's why I preferred to circulate close to the place designated by her for our next meeting. After a couple of hours I felt intense hunger and fatigue, so I left the Ca d'Oro for a while and proceeded along a dark, cramped *vicoletto* * where, dropping into a little café on the corner of Vittorio Emanuele, I downed a cup of coffee in a single gulp. A few minutes later I stood again on the boulevard, casting an impatient glance in the direction from where Inez's gondola would appear.

Finally, Inez arrived. Sweet, olive-skinned, stunning. When I wanted to her help get off, she shook her head:

"We will continue on in the gondola. Please sit by my side."

And she pointed to a place in the boat.

"*Beppo, cava il felze!*" she commanded her gondolier.

And while the servant was fulfilling the command by rolling up the silk canopy over our heads, she leaned on my shoulder and, looking at me playfully in the eye, asked:

"Did you think of me at least once since our parting?"

"*Señora*," I said, sinking my eyes into hers, "I am bewitched by you."

"That is good; that is the way it should be. *Avanti*, Beppo!"

"Where are we going?" I instinctively asked.

---

* A narrow street. (Author's note.)

18

"In the direction of Fondamente Nuove using a system of crisscrossing canals. I love to move along in a gondola through these quiet water paths that wind between old houses permeated with dampness."

We bounded from the stop. Directed by the skillful paddle of the gondolier, the boat kept close to the shore, and shortly, after making an adroit roundhouse right, it left the Grand Canal and entered the narrow neck of the Rio di San Felice.

"*A—oel!*" came the warning cry of our rower. "*A—oel! Sia stali!*"

The gondola slipped under the bridge linking Victor Emmanuel Street and San Felice Square, and turned right again, this time into the Rio di San Sofia. Listening attentively to the splash of the paddle, we savored the quiet of the ride.

This excursion between tenements had a special charm. Despite the prosaic nature of life that emanated from the old low-rise shabby houses with clothes hanging to dry here and there on perches and ropes, something mysterious existed in this atmosphere. Something was hidden in murky arcades lit poorly by tongues of gas flames, something was lying dormant in the dark courtyards, peering here and there through patterned gates, lurking in dirty pools stale for years. Once in a while, a human head would lean out of a window, and a pair of eyes, passionate and of the south, would look out and disappear, as if frightened at the sight of strangers; once in a while a marvelous song flowed out from the mysterious depths of an apartment, suffused with longing, and it reverberated *arpeggio* between the walls of the houses to become silent, ashamed of its untimely beauty.

In the dark, dense, still waters the upside-down reflections of houses were joined in a trembling embrace; dirty-greasy strands and spume swirled, glittering in the light. In places, emerging from the mass of homes and buildings, were covered galleries suspended in the air—"bridges of sighs" of grey, sad everyday life—and like hands reaching over a precipice, they joined both sides of a canal. Elsewhere, the arch of a stone vault, spanning the surface of the water with its underside, would shift its willowy spine from recess to recess.

The quiet of the little streets was interrupted from time to time by the cries of the gondoliers.

"*Sia premi!—Sia stali!—Sia di lungo!*" they called out, avoiding each other at the turns.

At the Rio di San Andrea we had to stop for a while, as a number of boats had crowded into a narrow strip of water, creating a bottleneck behind a pot-bellied freight boat loaded down with coal that could not extricate itself from the crush. Finally the freighter rubbed against the boulevard with its side, extricating itself out of the trap, and the passage opened up. We sailed onto the St. Catherine canal.

"To the left, Beppo! Under the *ponticello* arcade!" the *Doña* told him.

The gondola swam up to the debarking stairs. We got out. The lady turned to the gondolier:

"Wait for us in ten minutes by the Fondamente Nuove stop."

"*Sta bene, signora, sta bene.*"

And while Inez, supported by my arm, went up the

steps to the shore, the old gondolier went farther along the canal to then turn to the north and exit, through the Sacca della Misericordia, onto the wider waters of the New Jetties. Meanwhile, we passed by the churches of St. Catherine and the Jesuits and plunged into the labyrinthine alleys of Venetian suburbs.

The afternoon sun, leaning slowly toward the west, flooded with gold the square pavement tiles and shone straight into our eyes.

"How cheery it is here, how sunny!" exclaimed Inez, whose straight, elegant figure threw off a strong and long shadow behind her.

"Particularly after those dark, cavernous canals," I added to her observation.

And as best I could, I tried to drive away with small donations dirty, ragged children, who had been accompanying us stubbornly for some time already.

"*Un baiocco, bella signora, un baiocco ai poveri bambini!*" whimpered a skinny freckled girl on behalf of the others.

Doña Orpega took out from her bag a dozen half-lira pieces, wrapped them in paper and, laughing, threw the packet up into the air. With a clatter, the money scattered about the decorative pavement.

"Let us get out of here while they are occupied in picking up the coins."

We eagerly veered into a neighboring alley. A few steps in front of us glittered the brilliant lagoon.

"We're here. The Fondamente Nuove in the full glory of a July afternoon."

Stretched out into the distance the boulevard was littered with people. At tables set in front of wine and pastry stores, people were sipping sweet-tart Marsala, tourmaline chianti, purple grenadine or robust *nostrano* from nearby vineyards. Gondoliers in orange shirts and wide, black hats solicited passers-by with proposals of trips to Lido, the islands of San Michael, Murano, Burano and the charming *isola di* San Francesco del Deserto. Beppo, smiling and happy that he had been able to anticipate us, was already waiting in a pictur-esque pose, leaning on his paddle at the top of his *Rondinella*. I turned a questioning look at Inez. And she, stepping down into the boat, graceful and elegant, in a tight satin dress the color of *bleu foncé*, pronounced the aim of our trip in two words:

"San Michele!"

"To the Isle of the Dead?" I asked, taking a place next to her in the gondola. "Why exactly there?"

She looked up at me with a surprised expression.

"Were you already there perhaps?"

"No, I wasn't," I replied, looking at her thoughtfully. "You see, *señora*, I do not like cemetery retreats."

"But it is worth going to see. There are apparently sev-eral Polish monks in the monastery nearby. Are you adamant about not going?"

"Not at all," I denied. "How can I resist your wishes? *Avanti, signor gondolier, avanti!* It is just a little unpleasant for me that we are starting our excursion at this place."

"*Por Dios!*" she said, shading us both with a parasol be-fore the intrusive rays of the sun. "I do not like men who exaggerate. *Adelante, Beppo! Sia di lungo!*"

The gondola bounded from the shore. The waves, cut by the broadsword of the paddle, sparkled in a myriad of lights and swirled about the boat.

"This clean water, refreshed constantly by the sea, is quite bracing," I said, breaking the silence with my observation.

"It's so different than the lazy, thick and fetid water of the canals."

"Yet there is something mysterious in that water. If one can speak of the soul of the Venetian lagoon, it hides in that black, slumbering deep water suffused with effluvium."

"Look there!" she interrupted, pointing to the right. "What a picture! Inspiration for a painter!"

Nearby, weighed down to half its broadside, sailed a barge under the triangle flag of Lacjum. She was taking vegetables from the gardens of the island of Le Vignole to the Venice market and fruit from the orchards of its neighbor, the green Torcello. The canvas of the lemon-yellow sail, with the image of the patron, St. Mark, billowed out gently from the gusts of the western wind over mounds of red-brick colored tomatoes, pyramids of carrots, beets, turnips and cones of grapes, peaches, plums and olives.

"Colors as if from Claude Monet's palette."

"Or our Wyczolkowski."

Farther on, the white outline of a cemetery wall could be seen.

"Somewhere close by," explained *Doña* Inez, "is where the city government orders a bridge of boats spread out between Venice and St. Michele Island during All Soul's Day for the convenience of the populace."

The gondola moved alongside a wall laved by gently sloshing waves and curled into the harbor in front of the monastery. We got out and, going through the abbey gate of the Order of Franciscans, entered the cloister. Inside, we could see several monks strolling between pillars. Their dark figures, framed in the rough lines of their habits, contrasted clearly against the sun-lit background of walls, columns and floors. Emerging from the wide sleeves of their religious attire, the monks' hands passed along rosary beads or, with fingers plunged into breviaries, were flipping through pages, creating a light rustling. From the interior of the basilica, on the left side of the cloister, came the scent of incense and burning candles; from the depths of the atrium, from the lovely Capella Emiliana, came the sweet tones of a harmonium: someone was playing Gounod's "Ave Maria."

We passed through a colonnaded-enclosed courtyard and, going through another gate, emerged onto the cemetery. It was six o'clock. Flooded with streams of the sunset, the refuge was basking in gold and white—the gold of the sun and the white of the marble. For a moment I shut my dazzled eyes. We walked along a cemetery wall inlaid with inscribed slabs, burial cavities and niches. Under our feet an underground chamber rumbled dully; to our side glared blinding reflections from the sun's rays.

"How little greenery is here!" I said in a complaining tone. "What a desperate drought of anything but white! Indeed, *señora*, this despotic, all conquering whiteness is terrible. It seems to me almost physically painful."

She looked about, slightly raising her eyebrows.

"You speak as a son of the North. Your cemeteries must have a completely different look?"

"Oh, yes. Our places of eternal rest have plenty of trees and bushes. Profuse, lush greenery separates the houses of the dead, covers the deadly white of tombstones and mausoleums with festoons of ivy, flowing birch bushes and viburnum. In the Polish cemeteries Mother Nature wraps the shrines of death in her maternal arms—while here in this blessed, eternally smiling land of the sun, even in this refuge of the dead, art ruthlessly exhibits its cold, marble triumph: a sorrowful triumph of whitewashed graves. Oh, how I miss vegetation here!"

I stopped at one of the tombs, which suddenly attracted my attention. I was struck immediately by its original composition.

On a terrace before a house stood a life-size statue of a woman with gentle appearance and full of sweet femininity. With her left hand she was gathering up the folds of her dress, while in the right hand, raised in a graceful gesture, she was carrying a pot of flowers.

"*A Luisa Riccardi, moglie adorata—il marito,*" I read the inscription at the bottom.

"This is the grave of a Venetian patrician," Inez explained to me. "She died a sudden violent death. Her distraught husband ordered the figure of his beloved solidified at the moment when she was leaving the house for a walk in the garden: that is how he apparently saw her for the last time— that is how he saw her a few hours before her death. That moment is immortalized in marble by the sculptor."

"How beautiful, *señora*," I said thoughtfully.

"And maybe that is precisely why it is adjacent to another beautiful carving," she said, advancing toward the next tomb. "What have you to say about this grave?"

On a disc of alabaster stood out two torsos *en relief*: a young man and a bewitchingly beautiful woman. His enamored eyes were fastened on her, as he was extending his thirsty lips toward the goblet she was presenting to him with a smile. Involuntarily, a suspicion was created that the cup contained poison. Because in the woman's smile lurked a hint of deceit and cruelty. But the blinded man appeared not to notice this—and he certainly did not see the narrow Venetian dagger that she held in her other hand, behind her....

I glanced at the inscription on a marble ribbon.

"*Al suo adorato sposo, Don Antonion de Orpega, spento supremo piacere nel—la moglie*"—this particular tomb confided to the world its secret in these concise, lapidary words.

I looked at Inez, shaken to the core.

"So here lies—"

"My husband," she finished with a strange smile that was new to me.

And only then, from this smile of hers, did I realize that she was the woman on the slab.

"Let us sit down on a bench in the cypress alley," she suggested.

I obeyed, full of conflicting feelings. We sat in a niche surrounded by cypresses. For a moment, there was silence between us. Long shadows from sepulchral guards lay at our feet in sharp outlines and blackened the golden gravel paths with hieroglyphics of death. From somewhere inside the cemetery came the clatter of a stonemason's hammer at work over a new headstone, answered by the sound of organ vespers....

"My husband committed suicide," I suddenly heard her alto voice, "in the fifth year of our marriage."

"So you pushed your husband into the arms of death, *señora*," I replied, almost sharply.

"From where comes this prosecutorial tone?" she asked, tapping me lightly with the end of her flaming umbrella. "Do not forget yourself. Besides, he passed away in the highest ecstasy of happiness; he died for me and because of me. Is that not beautiful?"

Is this a monster or is she mad? I thought. But looking at her, I completely forgot about any ethical considerations and just took in her diabolical beauty. Meanwhile, she said in an even and calm voice, as if she was talking about someone she had known only by hearsay:

"It happened unexpectedly. So unexpectedly, so suddenly, as happens sometimes with happiness or death. And it is precisely in this that I see the most beautiful theme of this story. For you must concede that I deserve my life to be filled with exceptional moments."

And she gave me a defiant look. She was too beautiful not to admit her right. So I lowered my head in silence and continued to listen.

"It was on one of those lunar nights, one of those Venetian nights full of mandolins, that *Don* Antonio de Orpega said, cradling his impassioned face between the mounds of my breasts:

" 'You have given me the greatest happiness tonight, Inez; I don't know if I can survive it till the dawn.' "

" 'Ha, ha, ha!' I laughed thoughtlessly, caressing his manly beauty."

" 'You are pathetic, my handsome husband!' "

" 'You don't believe me, Inez?' "

" 'I don't, Antonio. You desire me too much to part so easily with life now.' "

" 'You don't believe me?' he asked again, a touch of insanity in his lovely, unforgettable eyes."

" 'Come to me, Antonio! After all, we're just people, just a pair of lovers hungry each other.' "

" 'Then I will prove it to you.' "

"And he left the bedroom. A moment later, a revolver shot ended the poem of his life. *Don* Antonio de Orpega, my husband, was a beautiful person—is that not so, my dear friend?"

"He loved you, as no one else on earth can love a woman," I replied softly.

"Yes. This was a *l'amore altissimo—l'amore supremo.* And that is why he feared that one day in the future I would not be there to stand at his grave. While there was time, he departed into the shadows of the underworld because he did not want to outlive his great emotion. He was a genius of love."

"I admire the both of you; him for his passion and you for your objectivity."

"My feelings," she said haughtily, "are exclusively my own.

28

For someone else I think it is appropriate to talk about the incident only as an exceptional work of art. You may want to look at them and evaluate them from this point of view, my dear friend."

"I will do as you say, *señora*, though you should understand that I did not request these confidences."

And I got up from the bench. Without saying a word, she extended her hand in a sign of agreement. I pressed it to my lips and said:

"It is late already and the guard is calling people to leave the cemetery."

And, in truth, a man was signalling to us from the farther end of the alley as he approached.

"Yes, it is time to go back," she admitted thoughtfully. "The cemetery closes early here."

Soon the gondola was sailing again along the lagoon.

"Where are we going?" I asked, my glance sliding along the water.

"To the Riva degli Schiavoni. I want us to listen to the orchestra concert at the Café Orientale and follow the evening movement by St. Mark's Pier."

"A most beautiful section of the city," I replied, turning serious all of a sudden.

She tapped me on the arm with her fan.

"Why so thoughtful now?"

"The aim of our trip has provoked in me some sad associations. I will tell you about them when we get there."

"Very well. Meantime, throw of your unhappy meditations and enjoy the view."

Inez was right: the beauty of the lagoon was compelling with elemental power. The gondola rounded the eastern tip of Venice, and passing by the docks of Arsenal, it squeezed into the canal between St. Peter Island and the city itself. A wave, slit by the gill of the paddle, sloshed gently against the side of the boat and, repelled from the black hull, left in a thousand ripples to the shore. When we passed the cape of Punte di Quintavalle, a big, burly wave came from somewhere and rocked gondola heavily. Inez glanced at Beppo with concern.

"That's a *piroscafo* from Torcello on the way to Ponte del Vin. Its belly ploughed through the lagoon and hurled a mass of water under us, causing the boat to rock," explained the boatman.

We exited out into the deep waters between the island of St. Helena and the Public Gardens. From a distance, the sound of music could be to be heard. Along strewn gravel and the sand of the boardwalk, of which a narrow ribbon wrapped around Punte della Motta, strolled several couples. From the bushes that buttressed the garden, constantly kissed by the waves of the lagoon, leaned out the resolute bronze bust of Richard Wagner.

"One has to admit," I noted, "that the choice of this place for this bust was very apt. It seems as if the ghost of the creator of 'The Flying Dutchman' is constantly leaving with the waves to tantalizing distances...."

We sailed onto the wide waters of the Canale di San Marco. Before us the wonderful panorama of the harbor was spread out. Countless gondolas and boats winged with yellow or the color *terra cotta* frolicked about the surface of the lagoon. From everywhere, as if to the central point of gravity, vessels headed to the harbor, flapping in the wind a parade of banners and flags. Here sailing triumphantly from the porto di Lido was some sea giant boasting from afar the colors of Albion. There, after stopping at the Adriatic gateway in the port of Malamocco, rose on the horizon of the bay a French frigate as graceful as a sylph. Elsewhere, in the narrow passage between Giudecca and the island of San Giorgio Maggiore, a passenger steamer moved along on the way back from Chioggia.

Beppo, taking in with a loving glance his native city and the lagoon, began to sing the immortal "Santa Lucia." The gondola reached the pier. A few beats of the paddle, a few agile turns among the maze of ships—and we came to the della Paglia bridge.

"Beppo," said *señora de Orpega* to the gondolier in parting, "you are free the rest of the day. I will return home on foot."

And, with my assistance, she got onto the marble waterfront.

"We are going to the Café Orientale."

As usual, this time I took in with delight the snow-like wonder of the Doge's Palace, ran thoughtful eyes over the Bridge of Sighs, along the grim block of the criminal prisons and stopped them *"on this long recess of granite, with green intermittent canals and cemented white bridges, where several thousand ships dock"**—on the Riva degli Schiavoni. And

---

* Excerpt from Cyprian Kamil Norwid's "Menego." (Author's note.)

suddenly, in the midst of the splendor of hues and colors, in the midst of this divine profligacy of beauty, breathtaking in wonder and continuous delight, I felt a tremendous, boundless sadness.

But this sadness *"did not belong to me."** Its funereal, black veils came to me from the perspective of another time, flowing from waves of returning echoes from the experiences of the great poet-loner, who here, on this same coastline, *"under the aurora of the evening sky,"* walked once in silence and *"withdrawn deep within himself"*....

And when afterwards, having taken my place at one of the café tables by the side of the beautiful woman accompanying me, I surveyed the purple sunset of the bay with eyes stunned from the glare and lights, the words of this forgotten poet about this place came to me again, saying:

"There, during matins in the mist, small fishing vessels depart... There, in the southern light, one sees the mysterious colors of Veronese, Tintoretto, Titian.... There, in the light of the moon, vessels disappear into the great darkness, and where the moonlight silvers the waves, the glittering cleaver at the gondola's bow, attached to a toothed profile, reveals itself..."

Inez's voice roused me from my thoughts:

"Perhaps now you would like to share you unhappy reflections with me, which the Riva degli Schiavoni apparently elicits. Let me remind you of your promise."

---

* Quote from Cyprian Kamil Norwid's story, "A Handful of Sand." (Author's note.) Both "Menego" and "A Handful of Sand" address aspects of death in a melancholy manner. (Translator's note.)

"And I will faithfully keep that promise."

I drank my black coffee, lit a cigarette, and said, gazing in the direction of the Doge's Palace:

"This way, along the same waterfront, which smiles proudly to the rising sun with the whiteness of its marble, at this same time when the day is dying, walked, eighty-three years ago, a brilliant creator of symbolism in Europe before Maurice Maeterlinck, a Polish poet familiar to his own countrymen, a maternal descendant of Sobieski—Cyprian Kamil Norwid. And accompanying him along the evening promenade full of sad impressions was a certain Tytus Byczkowski, a painter, also a Pole, who during his bath on the Lido the next morning, *'went far into the waves'* and apparently drowned accidentally. Byczkowski was about sixty years old. He studied first at the Academy of Dresden, then in Munich, *'everywhere easily succumbing to local traditions, with Slavic obedience to each school—a model of patience, self-denial and humility,'* and that's why on the eve of his death he was finishing a small painting representing a fisherman with his children, a fisherman who labored the entire day to hold, by the evening, *'in his hand one prize—an empty seashell.'* So these two Polish wanderers, so unlike each other—one, born a creator, the other, a Slavic slave—strolled during the evening hours of 1843 along the coast of dei Schiavoni, *'or as one not yet faded inscription stated'*: Riva dei Slavi, or The Shore of the Slavs.

"They talked about Art, and as they were coming down from the Ponte della Paglia toward the *piazzetta*, Byczkowski drew attention to the wealth of creativity in the architectural details that comprise the Doge's Palace, turning, in a strange circumstance, the entire conversation to the topic of inspiration and originality, which were precisely lacking in his own creative endeavors.

"And then the great creator of *Promethidion* explained to him that the immortal in Art is only that which is begun in devotion and that the true form of beauty is love."

"And then, my dear friend?" Inez interrupted my momentary silence. "And then?"

"And then they went down to St. Mark's Square, where it was already twilight, and where *'around the square it began to get noisy, the cafe lights came on, and people waited for the music from a military band, usually* (in those days) *from Czechoslovakia, performed here in the evening.'* To one of these cafés, undoubtedly somewhere along the Procuratie Vecchie, they entered..."

"And the next day Byczkowski was dead," finished the *Doña.*

"Yes. He went to the bottom of the sea—like Hjalmar's daughter in Ibsen's *The Wild Duck**—he went down into the depths with the realization of the agonizing truth of his life. *"Verily, this world is sad until death..."*

I became silent and, lost in thought, gazed at the darkening file of gondolas, boats and motor boats at our feet. Meanwhile dusk fell completely. As if from a sign given by the invisible hand, the electric arcs of bulbs, cloches and lanterns

---

* The reference here is to Gregers' line in the Ibsen play when Hedvig's suicide is discovered: "In the depths of the sea..." (Translator's note.)

were suddenly lit up, while from St. Mark's Square flowed a band serenade; Venice was celebrating the evening with a nocturne of praise. Over the lagoon began to wander to and fro will-o'-the wisps. Opposite the pier some warship at anchor before the island of San Giorgio Maggiore, all dressed up in flags and banners, lit up the name of its admiral in a birthday celebration. From the Punta della Salute, on the other side of the channel, soared into the sky spindle rockets, bursting into a shower of sparkling fiery fountains and bouquets. Along the Lido coast a long line of lights and sconces burst forth with illumination....

I tore my eyes away from the bay and met Inez's searching gaze. I withstood it calmly for a moment. Suddenly, out of nowhere, a question occurred to me:

"Do you believe in omens?"

She seized my hand and responded in amazement:

"What made you say this just now? Do you know how to read other people's minds?"

"The question came to me out of the blue; I couldn't suppress it. Sometimes a thought arises from somewhere and it's not known why."

Animated, she contradicted me:

"Oh, no! In this case you are mistaken. At the moment you asked me that question I was thinking about the old Gypsy woman from Asturias who foretold the early death of my husband."

"So your thought transferred itself to me," I concluded.

All of a sudden we heard, in English, the distinct fragment of a conversation from a neighboring table: *"Do you know anything about Luigi Bellotti, the painter-medium?"*

Two men were sitting at the table. One of them was attired in a striped suit, a monocle in his eye, and with the characteristic clean-shaven face of an Englishman, while the other gentleman emphasized his affiliation with that tribe to a far lesser degree.

"How strange," stated the *Doña*. "That conversation of our neighbors that we just heard is as if a continuation of the subject we are interested in, and also a reminder to me."

"What has the painter Bellotti to do with what we were talking about?" I asked.

"You haven't heard of him?"

"No."

"He is a phenomenal medium who in a trance, blindfolded, paints pictures that mimic the manner of the old Italian masters. I recently read an interesting article about him in *La Tribuna*."

"I still don't see the connection with what we were talking about."

"You will in a moment. Bellotti is also reportedly in contact with the afterworld, and, as he maintains, he hears voices of the dead from time to time."

I looked at her with a tinge of irony:

"Don't tell me that you believe in these 'spirit' fairy tales?"

"Then let's call them a symbolic expression of the medium's subconscious, if you will. In any case, after reading the article in *La Tribuna*, I decided I would have to pay Mr. Bellotti a visit. I expect that will tell me something about my future from these 'voices.'"

"Ah, now I understand—this is also a type of divination."

"The conversation of those two men reminded me that I intended to visit Bellotti. I want to go in the coming days. You will go with me, yes?"

"How so? Does Bellotti live nearby?"

"He is always in Venice. He lives on the Calle della Rosa. So, will you accompany me?"

"With the greatest pleasure. For a certain while, I see unusual events unfolding before me. "

"It happens in life that after a period of dullness and commonplace reality a series of exceptional incidents follow. For me, some inner voice is telling me that I am living on the eve of incidents that will determine my fate. Who knows, perhaps my acquaintanceship with you, *Signor Polacco*, is the first link in the chain."

"I don't think so," I replied with a smile. "That would be too flattering for me."

"What modesty! I do not believe in it at all. You men are all born hypocrites in relation to us."

And she attacked me with the brilliance of her eyes. In this manner we spent the evening talking and didn't even notice when the café clock struck ten.

"*Por Dios!*" she cried suddenly, realizing what time it was. "I have to return home."

And we went along the *riva*, then through the pier. We rubbed up against the crowds lingering at the *piazzetta* and the marble square in front of St. Mark's Church, until, passing under the arch of the Torre dell'Orologio, we entered the Merceria.

Despite the late hour, the city was vibrant with life. It seemed that its pulse was beating even stronger now than during the day under the blistering sun. From the open shops, cafés and restaurants the glow of lights flowed to break apart mysteriously in the dark waters of canals large and small. Tenants, merchants, caretakers of houses and vendors, especially women and children, turned out in crowds, escaping the stifling heat of their flats, and sat at gates and entrances—points of observing the night traffic and bonfires—the forge of small-town gossip. Because Venice—this beautiful Venice, this Venice admired by the cultural world, with its palaces, museums and galleries, is nonetheless a province. And that may be its special charm, this unique alignment of the high culture of centuries with the simplicity and unpretentious of a small town. That's why a foreigner feels better in Venice than, for example, in Florence or Rome, where he can feel weighed down at times by monumentalism and a culturally "official" environment. And I loved deeply this pearl of the Adriatic precisely for her "*desinvolture.*" Despite her incomparable beauty, Venice allowed me to feel at ease and did not force me to stand on artificial and tiresome ceremony.

Sharing each other's observations and insights on this city of lagoons, we passed the Ponte Rialto, the Malibran Theatre, Scuola dell'Angelo Custode and entered the always bustling Calle Vittorio Emanuele.

"How wonderful is it that there is no place here for automobiles, that plague of the 20th century," remarked Inez.

"This beautiful city soothes my ruffled nerves for two months every year."

From the Calle di Traghetto, we plunged into a system of narrow cross streets heading toward the Grand Canal. Here it was considerably quieter: the night movement, centered in the main artery streets of Victor Emmanuel and Lista di Spagna, was considerably muted in these coastal offshoots. Only here and there the figure of a lone pedestrian moved among the shadowy twilight of tenements, only here and there did a cat, emaciated and feral, dart across our path.

At the exit of one of these alleys, the so-called Calle dei Preti, or the Street of Priests, a group of children were playing by the wall of the house. A lantern above the archway spread an anemic circle of light over them and with difficulty transported its radiance to the neighboring little plaza. Suddenly, a panic arose among the children. The song they were singing stopped midway, the hands joined in a dancing procession fell down, and the frail, emaciated figures lined up with backs against the wall of the building.

"*Donna Rotonda passa! Donna Rotonda!*"*—we heard the fearful whispers.

On the square plaza between the streets, the fantastically elongated shadow of a woman, coming from the depth of an adjacent alley, appeared. She was tall and held herself stiffly like a column. A bell-shaped hat, *à la* Lindberg, pulled halfway down her forehead, with hanging belts at the cheeks and a neck lining, shrouded her head so tightly that it gave the

---

* "Lady Rotonda (The Round Lady) is passing by." (Author's note.)

impression of helmet with a slightly raised visor: from a small rectangular cut-out at the front could be seen a fragment of a snowy-white face, as if frozen from frost, with tight, thin stubborn lips. A portion of this motionless and severe face, like a mummy's or a Greek tragic mask, was not enlivened by any expression, for the eyes were carefully shielded by the edge of the hat that hung over the eyebrows. If not for the certainty and determination of her movements, one would have supposed that *Donna Rotonda* was blind.

Her bizarre appearance was intensified by an unfashionable, antiquated outfit: a tight corsage with bouffant sleeves the color of burnt sand and that matched the color of her crinoline dress. This dress, as lengthy and wide as a shadow, and mercilessly dusty and ragged, to which *Rotonda* undoubtedly owed her sad-funny nickname, trailed behind her on the ground with a soft, particular rustling.

Upright and cold as a tomb stele, she walked with a calm, even step, holding with both hands on her right shoulder a slender vessel, similar to a Greek amphora.

"She's mad," Inez explained when *Rotonda* disappeared around the corner of a church. "She lives somewhere near here. I come across her sometimes. Not a very pleasant neighbor."

"*Donna Rotonda*," I repeated thoughtfully. "The Round Lady. It's not surprising at all that she evokes such a panic among children. There is something disturbing about this unfortunate woman. She passed us by as if a symbol of suffering and ridicule intertwined in a tragic knot."

"I don't like to meet her on my way," Inez confided to

me quietly, as she tightened her grip on my arm. "If I see her from a distance, I head in a different direction if I can.... But I'm already at home. *Buena noche, caballero! Hasta luego!*"

She took a key out of her handbag and inserted it into the lock of a small inconspicuous door that comprised the side entrance to the palace opposite the shore. My lips clung to her hand for a long while. She gently stepped back and vanished inside the house.

I remained alone at the mouth of a street drowning in the twilight. A few steps away from me the waters of the *Grande Canal* splashed against the gangway steps; on the corner, farther on, a lantern was expiring. I walked away slowly toward the city, venturing into the labyrinth of streets, backstreets and alleys. I was not in a hurry to get to my lodging. The warm July night disposed one to romantic roaming. Reminiscing about the experiences of the day, I wandered a long time like a night-walker among the ravines of the buildings, in crisscrossing traps of Venetian *rughe* and *rughetti*, *corti*, *salizzade*, *sottoportici*, *rami*, *rioterra* and *sacche*.* Until wearied by my trekking and the rich atmosphere about me, I found myself at the gate of my quiet inn in the alley called Calle di Priuli.

My last impression, which struck me just before falling asleep, was of a mysterious and distinctive rustling. But this sound was not sourced in the reality of the moment—rather, it was the stubborn memory of the rustling sound that had been produced whenever *Donna Rotonda*'s gown touched the pavement street of dei Preti....

---

*Types of Venetian streets, squares and entryways. (Author's note.)

July 10th. A couple of days ago, Inez and I went to see Luigi Bellotti at his residence on Calle della Rosa. The visit made a deep impression on us both, one we haven't been able to shake off as yet.

The man who greeted us was not quite thirty, slim, very pale, with a broad, prominent forehead and an elongated oval face. In his somber eyes were seen stray flashes of a recent ecstatic experience. In fact, as he later confessed, he had just finished a "séance" with some French professor who had arrived from France to specifically conduct experiments with him.

Assuming that we wanted to see his paintings, he guided us around his studio with great courtesy and showed us a few landscapes that mimicked wonderfully the style of Segantini and several canvases signed by Ciargi and Maggioli. When I asked him how he explained his unusual abilities, he declared, without hesitation, that he considered himself a tool of the dead artists who direct his hand.

"Researchers into this phenomenon who've had scientific sessions with you take a slightly different view of this," I made the cautious observation.

"I know," he replied, "but I do not share their opinion and my internal experiences prove me correct."

When I informed him of the aim of our visit, he smiled and said:

"I doubt very much whether I will be able to fulfill your wishes. I do not occupy myself with fortune-telling, and the voices, which I sometimes hear, do not reveal anyone's future to me. At least that's the way it has been so far. Nevertheless,

I will try to get into a trance, to which I will give a special direction connected with the *señora*. I will need an object that has belonged to the *señora* for a long time."

Inez gave him her ring. He put it on the small finger of his left hand and, sitting down in a chair next to an easel on which was a newly stretched canvas, he tied his eyes with a black sash.

"Now I ask for a couple minutes of absolute silence," he said, leaning forward a little.

Inez and I sat side by side on a sofa and did not let our eyes go of him. A deep hush fell into the atelier. I clearly heard the murmur of the city, seeping into the interior through the open window, and the ticking of the clock on the opposite wall. Inez nervously clutched my hand. In this manner, ten minutes went by.

Suddenly Bellotti grabbed a brush and palette and began to paint. We approached the easel on tiptoes to track the progress of his work. It happened at a very fast pace, so that shortly one could make out the content of the painting.

Across the canvas the steel-blue sash of a raging river unfolded. Some large city occupied its right bank; an opaque sea of mist was on the left. Between the two banks the span of a bridge emerged. What a strange bridge! The left span, which came out from the tangled mist and haze, seemed to be their spectral extension; like them, it was hazy and blurred. The right span, issuing forth from a city vibrant with life, was solid and with clearly defined shapes.

One this bridge two people had a rendezvous: From the sea of mists emerged a man; from the opposite side, a woman. We recognized them. The apparition of *Don* Antonia de Orpega and the madwoman *Rotonda* came together at the border of two worlds. They stopped in the middle of the bridge and shook hands, as if in a sign of an alliance....

The painting was finished. The painter put aside his brush and began to speak in a drowsy monotone:

"I hear a voice from the left: 'We made a pact, my sister, in suffering. Joined in the brotherhood of pain, both of us victims of a great passion, we have come together here, at the border between life and death, for the last time today. Because your time is approaching, sister. A man who is to become a link between her and you has already arrived. Don't forget, sister, don't forget!....' "

Exhausted, Bellotti fell back into the arms of his chair. We stood in silence, staring at the enigmatic image and weighing the dark words we had heard....

Suddenly Bellotti grabbed the brush again and in a few vigorous strokes crossed out his masterpiece. The contours were rubbed out, the colors merged, and the canvas was now a cacophony of spots. Everything vanished like a dream.

The painter removed the blindfold from his eyes and, giving Inez back her wedding ring, asked:

"Well? Did either of you get a clue to the future from what I painted or said?"

I told him the subject matter of his painting and repeated the words he had spoken. He bent his head in thought and then turned to Inez:

"You are a widow, *señora*?"

"Yes."

"Then the wedding ring brought up a vision of your deceased husband."

"But how did *Donna Rotonda* find her way into the painting?" I asked, getting involved in the discussion. "And what kind of connection could she have with the *señora*'s husband?"

"Perhaps the *señora* had been thinking of this tragic woman recently?" Bellotti threw out the supposition.

"Indeed," she replied. "Not long ago, we both came across her on the street in the evening. I don't know why, but that meeting made a bad impression on me, more than it would have otherwise, and that night I thought about this insane woman more than I probably should have."

"All this is fine," I remarked, "but it doesn't still explain the symbolism of the rendezvous and the contents of the conversation."

Bellotti uncrossed his arms in helplessness.

"I don't know, I don't know anything," he repeated. "At that moment I was just a tool of unknown forces. Or perhaps—perhaps only their plaything…."

We thanked him and, deep in thought, went down to the gondola.

I spent that evening with Inez in the Giardini Pubblici. Here, in the refuge of the park, among the Greek columns of one of the art pavilions, I was presented with the favor of her first kiss. A couple of hours later I was cuddling her in my arms in one of the chambers of an old palace from the times of the Doges.

"It happened," she said to me, stretching sweetly her

wonderful, dark-skinned body on the medieval bed under a baldachin. "I could not resist any longer; you arrived as destiny...."

When, intoxicated with the euphoria of lovemaking and not believing my own good fortune, I slipped out of the side door of her house, midnight was striking. With unsteady steps I plunged into the alleys of Venice. At the corner of Calle della Misericordia, *Donna Rotonda* appeared. As we were passing by each other, she raised her head, as if wanting to read the time on a church clock. I saw her eyes at that moment. They are dark-violet, with a hint of steel and hopelessly sad. Beautiful eyes....

August 10th. For a month I've been the happy, supremely happy lover of *Doña* Inez de Torre Orpega. This woman is a hundred times more beautiful and more refined than I had thought. She is a master in the art of lovemaking. And at the same time she always knows how to preserve an aesthetic moderation and never falls into base licentiousness.

For a month we have been living like a pair of demigods in love, not much aware of our surroundings and not much concerned about the opinion of people. Our days are devoted to excursions. Every day we go to Lido Beach, bathe in the sea, and then visit the curiosities of the lagoon. We've already seen the glass factory at Murano and the renowned lace school on the island of Burano; we've talked with fishermen in the shade of the lovely Torcello vineyards and spent a few wonderful hours in the cypress groves on the island of San Francesco del Deserto. Such are our days. But I would not trade all of these for one of our nights. Because our nights are similar to the enchanting fairy tales of the East where rainbow mirages are embroidered on a canvas of continually forgotten reality. In the exotic parks of our love, alabaster lamps burn; bathed by the sleepy silver moon, rare birds sway on branches and swans in love glide along gentle waters.

Blessed be the night on the island of Chioggia, that one night in which we were free to spend as spouses under the same roof until the morning.

"*Un letto matrimioniale, signore?*" the question was heard from the affable hotelier as we entered, a question so natural and obvious that it excluded any doubts.

"*Si, signore, un letto matrimoniale,*" I replied.

And we were considered a married couple.

I do not know if it was the role that was involuntarily thrust upon us or the melancholy of the picturesque harbor in the evening that attuned Inez to a deep lyricism, which that night melted the precious metal of her passion. When, amidst kisses and caresses, I picked her up from the bed and walked around the bedroom, rocking her like a child, she put her arm around my neck and began to weep aloud.

"My love, my dearest husband!" I heard her whisper through intermittent sobs.

Around two in the morning, exhausted, she fell asleep on my chest. Never before or since have I seen her so tender....

Such are our nights.

This surfeit of happiness has disposed me to people in a kindly and conciliatory manner. I am understanding and compassionate. The law of contrast has now made me feel the unhappiness of others more strongly. The more so that life seems to show this unhappiness to me at every step. As if it feared that I would forget. As if it wanted to caution me. Almost every day it reminds me about this, sending out Rotunda to meet me.

Because this is how I now call the poor madwoman, the terror of the Venetian little ones and embodiment of the atoning spirit of the lagoon.

This unfortunate woman has awoken in me a genuine interest, and I've already gathered information about her. Rotunda's name is actually Gina Vamparone, and she is the daughter of one of the caretakers of the palaces along the *Canal Grande*. Once renowned for her beauty, she became insane when she was abandoned by some Venetian baron. Leaving the town of lagoons forever, this seducer left his palace to Gina as a memento, together with its furnishings. But her mother preferred to remain in a modest room in the interior of the annex and there live out the rest of her sad life by the side of the mad woman rather than move to the master's rooms. That is why the palace, not inhabited by anyone, is empty. Only Gina goes there from time to time to put it in order, dusting furniture and carpets. Apparently she does not consider herself as the owner, but as a custodian of the house and deludes herself with the hope that the master of the house will return and that she will then give him an account of everything.

A propos the Greek amphora, it is probably one of the souvenirs from her beloved—she carries milk in it every morning and evening for her mother.

These handful of details were collected by me from neighbors and acquaintances. They did not dampen my curiosity—on the contrary, they stimulated it. There is something in the form of her insanity, her facial expression and attire, which remains a mystery to me. Something draws me to her, and that is why for several days, in my spare time, I have been following Rotunda from a distance. Is this not a paradox? I, the happiest person in Venice, I, the lover of *Doña* de Torre Orpega, am secretly following the crazy daughter of a caretaker of a house! Is this the pity of a king for a beggar or a caprice of *Le Grand Seigneur* Fate? It is strange, laughable, but true. Yes! Gina Vamparone fascinates me....

August 30th. How did this happen? In what manner? How could I have allowed it to happen? Why, it's disgusting, absolutely awful!....

And yet it did happen and nothing in the world can change it. It was like this...

Yesterday, about eleven in the evening, I was returning to my lodging from Inez's home, as was my routine. The night was sultry, the moon full. I walked slowly, dreamily, still feeling in my veins the fire of love's raptures. At some *ponte storto*, whose highly-curved arch connected two banks, I stopped. Taking delight in the silence, I leaned over the railing of the bridge and gazed at the black water of the canal. Then I heard a rustling behind me. I turned and saw Rotunda. She walked across the bridge, a few paces from me, rigid and inert, the helmet-like hat drawn heavily, as usual, over her eyes, supporting with her left hand the amphora propped on her shoulder. She seemed completely oblivious to me, even though I was the only person in this area at this late hour. Perhaps she did not even see me. She passed by like a ghost and began to move away in the direction of San Felice.

Driven by curiosity, I followed her, maintaining a discreet distance. In this manner we reached another bridge, this one over the Rio di Noale, after which Gina turned to the left in the direction of the canal. I stayed in the shadow of a corner house, for she was now crossing an empty area flooded with moonlight. As soon as she disappeared out of sight around a building, I ran up quickly to shorten the distance separating us, and once again I had her in front of me by several steps. Now there was no doubt that she was returning to her place, to the palace of her lover.

Soon her figure disappeared into the darkness of its portico. Carefully, stealthily, I approached the first column, and hiding behind its shaft, I took in the courtyard with my eyes. It was rectangular, encircled from all sides by galleries in the Mauritian fashion. In the middle, surrounded by bouquets of ferns, a silver fountain drizzled quietly. At the other end of the peristyle I saw Rotunda, as she was vanishing from my sight.

"The lodging of the caretaker must be there," I thought. "She most probably lives there with her mother."

I was about to go away when she appeared again to me in the beams of moonlight. With a bunch of keys in her hand, she stopped in the middle of the courtyard and seemed to ponder on something. Then she went up the stairs on the right side.

Under cover of the shadows cast by pillars and columns, I reached the first storey, and through an open door, I followed her into one of the rooms. The interior was rendered in the style of the early Renaissance. Impressed at the outstanding paintings hanging on the walls, I almost betrayed my presence before the insane woman. Fortunately, she was busy exclusively with herself. I hid behind a screen next to an old-fashioned fireplace and, from this vantage point, watched her movements.

She stopped in front of a large standing mirror and threw off that bizarre hat from her head. Soft, golden-copper hair rolled down her shoulders in a shiny cascade. Then she changed the lighting. The interior filled up with soft, warm crimson light flowing down from a shaded chandelier.

She approached the divan in the middle of the room and quickly began to undress. As if by a magic wand, her figure became transformed. The dusty and dirty rags of her everyday dress fell off, the ridiculous crinoline disappeared, and in the bouquet of red light stood a luxuriant, ruddy-haired beauty. It was no longer *Donna Rotonda*, the grim bogeyman of children, the sad-vile specter of a slumbering lagoon—it was Gina Vamparone, the unfortunate child of Venice, blossoming in the refuge of the lonely palace into a beautiful woman, maddened by love. In her proud, royal nakedness, she had changed beyond recognition. Her face softened, her stern tight lips mellowed out, and her dark-purple eyes took on a soft luster. She was exquisitely stunning. Such women the divine Titian must have seen in this beloved city to later appear in his creative vision of *Donna incomparabile*....

Having satiated her eyes on her own beauty, she started to dress. But now she put on an outfit that was quite different. It was expensive and stylish, as if modeled on one of the women's portraits on the wall opposite her.

In the blue, brocade dress with a collar that opened up around the neck like a vase of lovely tulips, Gina was now a Lucrezia Borgia or a demonic Beatrice, who, under an incantation, had descended from the frame of a Renaissance painting. A flirtatious smile twinkled in her eyes, descending to lips that were seductively parted, and flowed slowly to the corners of her mouth. Perhaps she was remembering years of love and happiness? Perhaps she was repeating one of the scenes in which she was the protagonist? Perhaps it was he who used to dress her that way, styling her in the fashion of great Italian beauties?....

Seized by the bewitchment that exuded from her entire figure, I forgot about my precautions and, full of admiration and adoration, I left my hideout. At the sound of my steps, she turned her head and saw me. She drew back sharply, covering her face with her hands, then dropped them rigidly along the sides of her body and assumed the mask of *Rotonda*. Finally, under the strength of my gaze, her face turned, in shame, as red as a rose. Suddenly she held out her arms to me, and scorching me with the fire of her most wondrous eyes, she whispered in ecstasy:

"*Giorgio mio! Giorgio mio! Mio carissimo Giorgino!*"

Drawn by this summons, oblivious that it was the result of a tragic mistake, that in reality she saw in me the other person, I knelt before her, embracing her knees. Then I felt her tremble and sway in my embrace. Our lips met, and our bodies became intertwined in a frenzy of love-making.

When I came to and realized what had happened, I saw that Gina had fainted. I rushed to get water and began to revive her. As soon as the first course of blood brightened up her pale cheeks and, with a deep sigh, she opened her sad, astonished eyes, I ran away like a thief.

September 6th. A week has gone by since the memorable incident on the night of August 29th. Nothing appears to have changed. As before, Inez and I see each other daily, drinking from a common cup of bliss; as before we go by gondola about the lagoon and take excursions close to the Grand Canal or farther away. And, yet, something has crept into our relationship and has caused a barrier to come between us.

A couple of times Inez has caught me in deep thought for no apparent reason. Once, she became full of bitter reproach because several times during ecstatic lovemaking I gave impression of being distracted. But I have also noticed changes in her, though nothing that would indicate a coolness of her feelings toward me. These changes have a special character. *Doña* Orpega has become from a certain time fearful and nervous. The slightest rustling awakens in her an exaggerated fear, the faintest shadow assumes frightful dimensions. Lately, she seems to be constantly listening for something, waiting for something.

The other day, in the evening, she snuggled up to me, trembling. When I asked her what was the matter, she replied:

"I constantly have the feeling that someone is creeping quietly toward me or is lurking behind my back. At other times, I feel as if someone has set out to come here, but has stopped along the way. Yet whatever this person's intention, it has not been abandoned—it has just been delayed for an unspecified amount of time."

"But these are all childish thoughts, my dearest," I said, trying to soothe her. "You are a bit overwrought and probably, because of this, oversensitive."

"No, no, Adamello! You are mistaken. This is something completely different. It's precisely this uncertainty that makes me very nervous, this hesitation, this lack of decision."

"What decision?"

"I don't know. If I knew, I would not be afraid. Most menacing is the fear of something elusive. I sense evil around me, hostile whirlpools."

I shrugged and deliberately passed on to another topic. Besides, it seems to me that she almost always manages to disperse this morbid fear of the unknown. If not for these temporary, though very unpleasant moods, our lives would be like a park in full blossom in May.

During this time I've seen Rotunda just once. She seemed not to recognize me. She passed by as she always did, stern and indifferent, her eyes hidden under the helmet. I avoid her now and frequently return from Inez's place in a roundabout way....

September 10th. And yet, Inez was correct. Her fears are

becoming more tangible. Today I can say that they are justified to a certain extent. That is if one can fear anything from that poor, unhappy crazy woman.

Rotunda is hounding her! There is no doubt. For some time she has been hovering around her vicinity like an ominous owl; she seems to always bloom up in her way as if she were the flower of grief and mourning. She is not aggressive—not at all: she only passes by like an inexorable reminder. She never looks at us—though we sense very well that she knows about our presence, that she is seeking us out— or rather, seeking out Inez. And perhaps it is her very stony, contemptuous tranquility, her sophisticated indifference that unnerves my beloved the most. One cannot even defend oneself from her, because she never accosts or provokes one. Her entire power lies in that she passes one by. *Donna Rotonda che passa....*

She also likes to surprise one—startling one by appearing out of nowhere and when least expected. A few days ago, in the late evening, we were departing on the gondola from the Ca' d'Oro palace. Taken up with a conversation with Beppo, whom I was helping at the oar, I had turned my back to the coast and was following the points of light being reflected in the canal. Suddenly I felt Inez squeezing my hand nervously.

"What is it, *carissima*?"

"Look, look there—on the shore—it's her!"

I glanced in the direction she was pointing to and, indeed, Rotunda was standing right at the edge of the water, straight and lofty as a column.

"She must have come to the shore to bid us farewell," I

tried to joke, but glancing at Inez, I quieted down......

Another time, during my absence, Rotunda unexpectedly showed up at the Papadopoli Gardens where *Doña* Orpega was waiting for me. She emerged from among a group of trees so suddenly that Inez let out involuntarily a cry of horror. Fortunately, I arrived at that moment. That meeting strengthened my suspicion that *Donna Rotonda* is pursuing Inez.

She seems to completely ignore me, as if I did not exist for her. Is this just a maneuver of a jealous woman? But can I be certain that jealousy is at work here, that Gina is not driven by entirely different motives? Perhaps I am, indeed, only supposed to be a "link" between these two women, a link and nothing more? It is certain that she seeks contact only with Inez. And it is precisely this that seizes Inez with fright.

"I would never want to be alone with her, one on one," she confessed to me tonight at dinner. "I've always had some instinctive aversion to this insane woman, and now I am afraid of her outright as if she were a ghost. Yesterday, after you left, when I went for a while to the loggia on the ground floor to breathe in the evening coolness, *Rotonda* was trying to get to me by a gondola."

"That's impossible!" I disputed in a lively manner. "It's just your imagination. Would she be so bold?"

"I am certain that it was her. I recognized her by her attire, by that horrible half-helmet, by her hat. Her gondola had already reached the steps in front of this place and she apparently wanted to disembark here. Terrified, I fled to the interior of the house and locked the gate behind me. This is an audacious mad woman! You should not leave me alone for one second. I'm afraid, Adamello..."

September 14th. Yes, Rotunda is jealous of Inez! Jealous as if I were her beloved husband! I was persuaded of this from today's truly absurd incident at the Ponte di Rialto.

Inez and I went there at noontime to eye the increased crowds due to the fair and to look over the shops. The bridge was swarming with passersby, hagglers and buyers, particularly dark-haired, blue-eyed townswomen—Venetian *cittadine*—throwing side glances, dressed in black mourning dresses and traditional shawls and mantillas, and taking the lead in the boisterous and excited fever of the market.

We stopped in front of the stall of Signor Giuliano, who loudly and with emphasis was proclaiming the superiority of his necklaces. One of them, an oval string of pearls, appealed to Inez. I interrupted the huckster's praise for his product and asked about the price. He answered with artificial nonchalance, immediately doubling the cost, of course. I paid him, and we were ready to leave, when suddenly Rotunda rose up right beside *Doña* de Orpega as if from the ground. Before I could stop her, she snatched the necklace from Inez's hands and disappeared into the crowds surrounding us. It happened so suddenly that at first all of us just stood speechless. It took a moment or two before a storm of shouts broke out and blunt epithets were directed at the insane woman:

"*Ladra Rotonda! Ladra, ladra!*"

Several people even rushed to pursue the fugitive. On Inez's face, pale from horror, a smile appeared.

"*Lasciate la!*" she calmed down the outraged crowd. "*Lasciate la povera pazza! Non m'importa!*"

And then she said to me in an undertone:

"Let it be of use to her. In fact, I'm happy with what has happened. She can finally leave us alone."

The incident at the Rialto Bridge upset me considerably, and I became seriously concerned about Inez's safety. That very evening we decided to leave Venice and relocate to Chioggia. We intended to carry this out the following day in the afternoon. Because the steamship between Venice and that picturesque island at the southern end of the lagoon was leaving around five o'clock, and as the sailing would take about two hours, we expected to arrive at our destination before nightfall and find temporary lodging in one of the hotels. Afterward, I would rent one of the villas facing the Adriatic Sea and live there with Inez.

The arranging of our plans and preparations for the trip took us all evening and part of the night. Inez was in a lively mood and with sparkling bright eyes bid me goodnight as the midnight hour approached. We agreed that I would come for her the next day at three o'clock, and that we'd take a gondola to the embarkation point at St. Mark's Square. I went away with a feeling of relief and soon fell into a deep sleep.

The following morning I devoted myself to settling up matters associated with our move, and at noon I ate lunch at a *trattoria* on the Cannaregio. When I left the restaurant, it was two o'clock. Gripped already by the neurosis that the trip had elicited in me, I paced along the Calle Vittorio Emanuele several times, smoked a lot of cigarettes, and unable to wait till three o'clock, I had the first of the free gondoliers by the canal take me to Inez. When we arrived at the palace, I noticed at the stop a gondola tied to one of the blue poles. The boat did not belong to Inez and the gondolier slumbering on the bench was not Beppo.

"Does the *señora* have guests?" I asked him reluctantly.

The boatman yawned and, stretching lazily, replied with a strange smile:

"Oh yes, the *signora* has a guest—a rare guest."

When I walked up the steps, the curtain separating the balcony and the interior parted, and Rotunda came out. Seeing me, she quivered, but immediately gained control of herself and indifferently, with a stone face, began to pass me by. I boiled with anger.

"What are you looking for here?" I asked sharply. "Why are you roaming about this house?"

She put me off with silence and, descending the stairs, got into her gondola. The blade of the oar made a plopping sound, the water ruffled, and the boat set off eagerly toward the middle of the canal.

I rushed to the entrance and, pushing aside the drapes, burst into the vestibule. Here, on the floor by one of the columns, lay Inez on her back. In her chest, plunged to the hilt, was a Venetian dagger. Gina Vamparone had a sure hand, sure and reliable: she had stabbed Inez right in the heart....

And once again it is a beautiful, Venetian afternoon. The sun dances along opal waves and the countless air particles over the lagoon glitter everywhere one looks. And once again, as on the first day when I met her, I'm bound from the Fondamente Nuove with my beloved. And, as then, we sail once more in the same direction: toward the Isle of the Dead....

She rests in front of me at the bottom of a black gondola, sweet and serene, amid a cascade of violets and white roses, a smile on her alabaster face. She sleeps quietly and like a princess, rocking on the waves, while above her is the canopy of a sapphire sky.

I lean toward the small feet, clad in satin shoes, and cuddle and press them to my lips, as I hear that someone is weeping at the rear of the boat.... It is Beppo, our gondolier....

Venice, July 1927

Visit the Stefan Grabinski website:
www.stefangrabinski.org